NANCY WARREN

CAT'S PAWS
AND CURSES

A VAMPIRE KNITTING CLUB
NOVELLA

Ambleside Publishing

INTRODUCTION

When Lucy organizes a holiday knitting circle, it's good fun, until someone's murdered...

And the culprit must be one of the knitters...

Knitting an ugly Christmas jumper at Cardinal Woolsey's knitting shop in Oxford, is supposed to be relaxing. Until a knitter keels over. it's soon clear to amateur sleuth Lucy that murder's in the air and the culprit is one of the knitters.

This is a fun take on a classic closed room mystery. Of course, no room is every closed when vampires live downstairs. But are the undead knitters to blame? Or is there more to this Oxford knitting circle than lumpy Santas and light-up reindeer?

This is a shorter holiday whodunnit. It was previously published in the collection: *Six Merry Little Murders.*

More fun than an ugly Christmas jumper, this story is part of the *Vampire Knitting Club* series, though it can be read on its own. It's full of good clean fun, mysterious goings-on and holiday cheer.

If you haven't met Rafe Crosyer yet, he's the gorgeous, sexy vampire in *The Vampire Knitting Club* series. You can get his origin story free when you join Nancy's no-spam newsletter at NancyWarrenAuthor.com.

Come join Nancy in her private Facebook group where we talk about books, knitting, pets and life. www.facebook.com/groups/NancyWarrenKnitwits

CAT'S PAWS AND CURSES

here is a phenomenon that occurs all over the British Isles toward the end of December. It turns grown men into virtual toddlers and seems to bring out the fool in even the most serious people. I refer, of course, to the Christmas jumper. This is what we Americans would call a Christmas sweater, but for some reason in the UK, the uglier the sweater is, the better. Don't ask me.

It was one of the stranger of the British customs I was trying to understand.

I'd become used to living in Oxford now that I'd been in that beautiful city for more than a year, but I didn't think I'd ever become entirely comfortable with the Christmas jumper, even though I owned a knitting shop. There was plenty of business to be had in providing wool and patterns for those garish, cartoonish sweaters featuring things like Christmas puddings, reindeer, snowmen and elves.

Even places where you would hope your business would be taken seriously, like banks or dentist's offices, looked more like daycare centers when in the grip of Christmas jumper fever. There was something particularly disconcerting about having someone come at you with a dental drill while wearing a lumpy, bumpy bright red sweater with a badly knitted reindeer in the middle of it.

However, I was never one to turn down business and, at my grandmother's suggestion, I'd put together a few kits specifically for those who wanted to try making their own Christmas jumpers. My gran might be one of the undead members of the vampire knitting club that met twice a week in my shop, but she'd owned the shop before I inherited, and she liked to keep her hand in.

Since I was a novice shopkeeper as well as a novice knitter, I happily listened to her advice. She'd suggested we'd get more business if I offered classes on knitting such a jumper, but I decided to institute a Christmas knitting and crochet circle instead. This way, anyone could come along and bring whatever project they were working on without expecting me to teach them anything.

The knitting circle was immediately popular with customers who were knitting or crocheting presents for loved ones who lived at the same address. It was also a good chance to sit busily working away for a few hours on a project while chatting with other like-minded craftspeople.

And so, every Tuesday night between seven and nine, I invited any of my customers who wished to come and join me in the back room of my Oxford knitting and yarn shop, Cardinal Woolsey's.

There was a core group who came every week, and it was augmented by those who dropped in sporadically.

I had been slightly unnerved the first time Mabel and Clara had shown up for the knitting circle. They were both vampires who lived underneath my shop. There was a trap-door that led from the back room down into the tunnels that wind beneath Oxford. My downstairs neighbor vampires were all excellent knitters, having had years—and in some cases centuries—of practice. The vampire knitting club met after ten o'clock, supposedly two nights a week but in reality whenever they felt like it.

There had always been an unwritten rule that the vampires had to stay out of my shop when humans were about. Not that any of them were great rule followers, but I tried to separate the daywalkers from the nightwalkers as much as possible. Fortunately, my vampires weren't hunters any longer. They didn't have to be. They had their own blood bank to meet their nutritional needs, and they'd had a lot of years to perfect their way of life. They were sleek, well fed, and rich. Their biggest problem wasn't hunger. It was bore-dom. Knitting helped while away the hours of an existence that would last for a very long time.

However, Clara and Mabel had the same problem as knit-ters who lived aboveground. They were working on holiday gifts for other vampires and wanted them to be a surprise. At least, that was the reason they gave me for wanting to join the human knitting circle. I liked Mabel and Clara, and in theory they'd be a great addition to the circle, mainly because they were much better knitters than I and could answer any ques-tions or untangle any knitting disasters. Probably mine.

However, I had to have a few rules before I'd let them knit with humans. First, they couldn't knit at their normal speed, which was so fast I couldn't watch them without going cross-eyed. Also, they had to be careful what they said. Like most older people, Clara and Mabel liked to reminisce about their experiences. In the vampire knitting club, it didn't matter if Mabel talked about knitting stockings for wounded soldiers in World War I. Or if Clara talked about the chilblains she used to get on her feet from walking to school in the winters before central heating. I warned them that if they made so much as one slip, I would have to ban them from my Christmas knitting circle. They assured me that they understood, and so I allowed them to come.

That particular Tuesday, I had six customers who'd signed up for my knitting circle, plus Clara and Mabel.

In the run-up to the holidays, I'd had fun decorating the front of my shop. There were twinkle lights around the front window, and I'd hung stockings and absurd Christmas jumpers, as well as gift ideas for all the family, from knitted tea cozies to children's toys. Naturally, I left the basket of wools that my black cat familiar, Nyx, used as a cat bed when she felt like snoozing. Oh, yes, my familiar. I was also a witch. Not the smartest or most experienced witch in Oxford, not by a long shot, but I was learning.

I made sure, as usual, that I had locked the trapdoor leading down to the tunnels. It wouldn't stop a determined vampire; it was just a reminder that I had people in my back room who would be more than a little shocked if pale-looking creatures with cold hands came up through the floor.

It was quite cozy in the back room, where I ran my knitting circle. I hadn't decorated it as much as the front of the shop, but Theodore, a vampire who was also a very good scene painter, had painted me a trompe-l'oeil fireplace complete with flames and a fireplace mantel from which I hung four hand-knitted stockings, which I'd filled with crumpled newspaper to plump them out. That morning, I'd come down to find that he'd added a Dickens-style village on the other wall, complete with carolers in the street. When I looked closer, I saw Scrooge being frightened by Marley's ghost and dancing and feasting at Mr. Fezziwig's ball.

Theodore had promised to paint over the fireplace when the holidays were over, but I suspected I'd keep the Dickens painting, as it made me smile all day.

I'd added twinkle lights around the scene, adding another festive note to the normally dull space. I always served tea and cookies around eight o'clock, halfway through the knitting circle. Usually they were cookies from a packet purchased from the small grocery store at the top of the street, but tonight I decided to really get into the spirit of the season and offer my knitters home-baked cookies.

Since I lived above the shop, it was easy enough to leave my cousin Violet, who was also my shop assistant, in charge for an hour or so, slip upstairs and whip up some holiday treats. I decided to bake white chocolate chip and cranberry cookies. It was a recipe that my mom used to make back when we lived in Boston. Even though I was in my late twenties now, I still got homesick around the holidays. Mom and Dad were archaeologists working on a dig in Egypt, so it wasn't often that I saw them for Christmas. I'd made quite a few friends, though, since coming to Oxford and knew I wouldn't be alone for the holidays. Still, the cookies were a happy reminder of home.

I had to walk to the store to get the ingredients, and as I did I noticed that the wind was blowing so hard, I had to push the edges of my hand-knitted woolen scarf into the front of my coat to stop it from blowing away.

"It's a blustery day out there," the cheerful grocer

remarked as he rang up the butter, white chocolate chips and dried cranberries.

Blustery was an understatement. When I walked the block back to my shop, I had to push against the wind as though it were a heavy door.

CHAPTER 2

$\mathcal{I}$ was cheerfully whipping the butter and sugar together in the electric mixer when the mixer suddenly stopped mixing. Had I blown a fuse?

I looked around and realized that my computer had also turned off and the lamp in the corner was out. I went to the window and peered down on Harrington Street and noticed that all the lights in my block were out. That was weird. A power outage? I couldn't remember having one before. Just as I was wondering how long it would last, the lights came back on again and the mixer burped back to life.

I finished the cookies, then put them into the oven to bake and sat knitting as the aroma of baking began to fill the air. Nyx settled herself beside me on the couch, her black furry body warm against my side. It was a very pleasant moment. I wasn't much of a knitter, but there were moments when it felt very peaceful, with my hands making something beautiful (with luck) and my thoughts free to wander.

When the timer went off, I carefully took the cookies off the baking sheet and transferred them onto cooling racks and then put the second batch into the oven. The recipe made four dozen cookies. I'd take two dozen down to serve for our tea break during the knitting circle. I'd keep the rest in case anyone came to visit for tea and cookies. That's what I told myself, anyway, but I was pretty sure I'd eat most of them all by myself.

I found a red and green tin in the back of Gran's cupboard and put my freshly baked cookies into it once they'd cooled.

Cardinal Woolsey's closed at five o'clock as usual, but I was back down just before seven to get ready for the evening event. I closed the blinds in my front window so that people walking by on the street wouldn't think I was open for late-night shopping. I also closed the curtain that led into the back, making the back room seem even more cozy. It was a habit I had from the vampire knitting club, but I liked the sense of intimacy.

I greeted each of the knitters as they came in from the cold, sending them straight to the back room to get settled.

The first to arrive was Hudson Caine. Hudson was one of the youngest knitters who took advantage of my circle. He was a student at Christchurch studying some kind of complicated philosophy that I didn't even understand. He was intense and very, very tall, with spiky black hair. I guessed him to be a little younger than me, probably in his mid-twenties.

Hudson was from Liverpool and sounded like the Beatles. I didn't care if he did talk about complicated philosophical subjects I didn't understand; I could listen to him all day. He was knitting slippers for his whole family, each in a different color, and was trying to get them all done before he went home for his winter break.

Tonight he was going to start work on a pair of slippers for his grandmother. I thought that was a nice role reversal. He wanted some pretty pink wool, he told me, and I helped him choose it. We went for a vibrant color. Not the pale pink of a baby sweater but the deep color of a healthy rose or a peony. "She'll like those," he said, "they're proper antwacky."

I laughed. "Antwacky?"

"You know, old-fashioned like."

It wasn't a very big sale, as his grandmother didn't have large feet and he already owned the pattern, but I always made a few extra sales on the nights of the knitting circle.

Hudson took his wool and headed into the back room just as Joan Fawcett arrived. Joan leaned heavily on her cane, and her eyes looked shadowed with pain. I thought the cold weather might be affecting her. Joan was the same age my grandmother would be if she were still alive and had kept aging. That put her at eighty-two. She looked older, though, and careworn. She wore a green and black plaid skirt, thick black stockings and black orthopedic shoes. She'd knitted her black cardigan herself, and under it was a white blouse pinned at the throat with a cameo brooch. Her white hair was cut short, more for convenience, I thought, than style. She didn't come to the knitting circle to keep her projects a secret from her family. She was a widow who lived alone. I suspected she came in order to get out and see people. I smiled at her warmly and invited her to go through. I knew she didn't need more wool, as she'd bought a quantity the week before. Joan was crocheting a blanket for her great-granddaughter in Ireland.

Eileen Crosby came in next. The wind was blowing so hard it grabbed the door out of her hand, and it banged against the wall. She looked as though she had come straight from work. She was a solicitor in her mid-sixties with blond hair going gray that was beautifully styled. Beneath her heavy coat, she wore a red and black dress with a heavy chain of a gold necklace and shiny low-heeled black pumps. She looked tired. "Busy day?" I asked her.

Her mouth turned down in a grimace. "I'd have been there till midnight if I didn't have the excuse of your knitting circle to get me away from the office. Besides, I'm completely out of the pale blue cashmere." Eileen was knitting a sweater for her tiny grandson. He was her first grandchild, and she was so proud, she glowed. As I brought her the wool, I asked, "Any new pictures?"

I wasn't in much suspense about the answer. There were always new pictures of darling young Henry. Sure enough, she pulled out her phone, and I dutifully admired tiny Henry as he drooled, slept, and watched the black and white mobile dancing above his crib.

I was just ringing up her wool order when Priscilla Carstairs came in. Priscilla was over eighty and seemed to be the embodiment of healthy senior living.

Where everyone else had bundled up against the weather, she seemed energized. "What an invigorating breeze. It'll put the roses in your cheeks." She was as loose-limbed as a teenager and held herself so straight and with such fine posture that whenever she walked into my shop, I felt as though I must be slouching and pulled my shoulders up and back.

She was long and lean, and her thick silver hair was pulled back into a bun. She was dressed all in black from her cashmere turtleneck to the bottom of her wide-legged jersey trousers. She wore ballet flats as though she'd lived in ballet slippers for so many years of her life, she couldn't break the habit.

"Lucy, dear," she said, bringing a rush of cold air in with her, "wait until you see my latest creation. Oh, and I'll need some more of the gold embroidery thread for my little drummer's drum."

She and Eileen greeted each other, and then Eileen headed with her new wool into the back room while I found the gold embroidery thread.

Mabel and Clara came in together. Clara rubbed her eyes. They'd obviously just woken up from their day's sleep.

Apart from being slightly pale, which everyone was this time of year in England, they could pass for two average little old ladies. So long as they remembered not to talk about things that no living human could possibly remember, I was perfectly happy to have them in my knitting circle.

It was ten after seven and I was just about to lock up and head into the back room myself when Sarah Lawson rushed in. "I'm so sorry I'm late, Lucy. I hope you weren't waiting?"

"No, of course not. You're just in time."

Sarah Lawson was in her late thirties and, in her white down coat, she looked like a snowman. She was round everywhere, from her face to her belly. She often sounded short of breath and was usually the last one to arrive at the knitting circle. "I hope you don't mind—I brought my dinner with me."

There wasn't much I could say, but I didn't think that eating a greasy burger from a fast-food place was entirely conducive to knitting.

"Do you need wools or patterns or notions before we go in?"

She shook her head and patted her bulging tapestry bag. "I have everything right here. Including my dins."

"Go on in, then, and I'll be right there."

I poked my head out of the door and looked up and down Harrington Street, but I didn't see any likely-looking knitters scurrying toward Cardinal Woolsey's knitting shop. In fact, it was so windy and cold, there wasn't a soul on the street. I shut and locked the door. I left the Christmas lights on, though, as they looked so pretty from the street and would be festive when my knitting circle left. After they were gone, I'd have to remember to turn out all the lights.

Nyx had been snoozing in her basket of wools, but when I locked up, she rose daintily to her feet, executed a perfect cat's stretch, stepped out of the basket and leapt nimbly to the floor. I thought she would make for the connecting door so that she could go upstairs to my flat, but no, she walked right past and headed for the curtained doorway that led to the back room. She pushed the curtain aside with her nose and walked in.

I followed.

The knitting needles and crochet hooks were already busily at work. Except for Sarah's. She was unwrapping a hamburger.

Nyx made her way around the circle, stopping to poke her head into Joan Fawcett's open tapestry bag. When she walked by Hudson, he leaned down to scratch her behind her ears. She showed her approval by purring loudly. Then she rubbed against Sarah's legs before jumping onto Mabel's lap, turning around a few times until she found a comfortable spot and then settling down for a nap. It seemed that lying in my front window snoozing for hours had exhausted her.

We always began the vampire knitting club meetings with a show and tell, so it had seemed natural to begin doing the same thing with my evening knitting circle. It was fun to see people's projects grow, especially if they had time to work on them between meetings. There was an excitement as the date of gift-giving grew closer, and this added a touch of suspense and drama to what was normally a fairly staid activity. Would Joan finish her granddaughter's blanket in time? Would little Henry's sweater be too big? But at the rate he was growing, should Eileen not make it big? Could Hudson complete six pairs of slippers and still manage his schoolwork?

I was about to ask who wanted to go first when Priscilla Carstairs spoke up. She was eyeing Sarah Lawson with distaste as Sarah chomped into her fast-food burger. A cardboard container of french fries was propped somewhat precariously between her knees. "Really, Sarah, this comfort eating isn't helping. It certainly won't bring him back."

There was a terrible silence, and in the silence we heard Sarah swallow a bite of her burger almost like a gulp. It was one of those painful pauses where no one knew what to say. Priscilla looked around at us all. "Well. It's true. There is no point hiding from the truth. Sarah's put on about two stone since her husband left her."

The trouble with knitting circles was that they could sometimes be confused with therapy circles. Sarah had shared her troubles in her marriage while the needles clacked on. We all knew about Gordon Lawson's unkindness to his wife and how he'd threatened to pack his bags and leave her on more than one occasion. It sounded like he did this every time she disagreed with him. Then she'd back down and beg him to stay.

Eileen Crosby was sitting beside Priscilla and turned to her, looking severe. "Priscilla, what you're doing is called fat-shaming. In the workplace you could be disciplined for speaking to someone that way."

Priscilla made a tsk-ing sound. "That's what's wrong with the world today. Everyone's afraid to speak the truth. Sarah needs to stop moaning and feeling sorry for herself. She should get some exercise and eat sensibly." She patted her own flat stomach. "Look at me. Not an ounce of fat on me. It requires discipline to stay slim and a lifetime of denying oneself fatty foods, but it can be done. I only want what's best for the girl."

"This is the first food I've had all day," Sarah said, swallowing and speaking up in her own defense. "And he hasn't left me. We're in marriage counseling. I'm knitting him a Christmas jumper. It's got elves throwing snowballs on the front of it."

Yep, that should solve her marriage problems.

"I'm sure it will be beautiful," Joan said. Joan was sitting on Priscilla's other side. She and Eileen were like kindness bookends pushing against Priscilla's thoughtless cruelty.

I decided to get this meeting back on track. "While Sarah finishes her dinner, why don't we do our show and tell? Who wants to go first?"

No one volunteered, so I turned to the man sitting beside Sarah, casting pink stitches onto his needle. "Hudson. How did your dad's slippers work out?"

"Yeah. Great. The ol' fella's got big feet and all, but he likes to put them up of an evening and watch telly. I didn't bring them tonight, but this is the wool for me gran's pair. Shouldn't take as long as her feet are so tiny." He glanced around. "I only hope I get them all done in time. I've still got me Auntie Lizzie's to do. I'm thinking red for her as she's got such a temper." He made a face, and we all laughed.

Clara and Mabel were next. Clara was knitting a lace shawl in pale gray that I happened to know was for their undead friend Sylvia. Mabel was also an exquisite knitter but she didn't have the most sophisticated taste. She was working on a jumper featuring a snowman with a felt carrot nose and lumpy black "coal" eyes. She said it was for a friend, and I suspected it was intended for Theodore, who was sweet enough that he might actually wear it.

Eileen was sitting beside Mabel. She held up little Henry's sweater, which consisted of the back and half of one sleeve. "I'll have to burn the midnight oil to get this finished in time." Then she pulled out her phone. "I got some new pictures of the baby this morning. I'll pass them around."

"You'll finish in time," Sarah said. "Don't worry."

Priscilla passed the phone along, barely glancing at little Henry. "He'll hardly be disappointed if he doesn't get his sweater in time for Christmas. He doesn't know what day it is. His brain is the size of a tadpole."

hen we got to Priscilla, she said, "I've been busy this week. I finished four of my little tree ornaments." And she pulled them out one by one. Priscilla was a bit of a show-off, but no one could deny her ornaments were really lovely. Her reindeer were works of art. I wouldn't have known you could knit antlers that small if I hadn't seen it done. She had a fat Santa with a sack of presents on his back and black knitted boots, the little drummer boy, a crocheted angel, and tonight she was working on a crochet snowflake.

"Who are they for?" Hudson asked her while we all complimented her.

She looked surprised at the question. "They're for me, of course."

Of everyone in the circle, she was the only one who was knitting for herself.

Eileen Crosby stopped to rub her knuckles. "Oh, this arthritis. I'm determined to keep up my knitting, but in the cold weather I do feel it in my joints." She turned to Joan

Fawcett, whose walking stick was hooked over the back of her chair. "You're a fellow sufferer, I presume?"

Joan Fawcett shook her head. "No. It's an old injury. I had a terrible fall when I was seventeen years old. I've never fully recovered."

"Oh, how awful," Mabel said. "Was it in the war?"

Mabel had been turned during World War II. I'd warned her about referring to things she shouldn't be old enough to remember. I glared at her, but she was gazing at Joan Fawcett with interest, and I could tell she was ready to launch into stories about the 1940s. I caught Clara's eye and watched as she gently kicked her friend in the ankle.

Mabel jumped, glanced at Clara and then at me, as she realized what she'd done. She looked guilty. If she hadn't been a vampire, I know she would've blushed.

Joan Fawcett also glared at Mabel. "In the war? What war? I am eighty-two years old, not a hundred and two."

"No. Of course not. I don't know what I was thinking."

"And what are you working on, Lucy?" Eileen asked. I was grateful to her for turning attention away from Mabel's blunder. I was working on a bright red scarf. In truth, I had quite a few projects that I had begun and not finished for one reason or another, mostly because I made a mess of them. It was usually easier to abandon the project than to try to fix my own knitting. But I had high hopes for that scarf. It was done all in the same wool, and if I was careful, I could manage the stitch. I held it up. "It's a scarf I'm making. The stitch is called the cat's paw." It was supposed to be easy. It was an eight-row pattern that repeated, and when it was done, the result would be a beautiful lacy-looking wrap. The vampires were always knitting me beautiful things, and for once I wanted to knit something for my grandmother. Since she'd joined the undead, Gran had become a great deal more stylish, and I thought she'd be thrilled to receive something I'd knitted myself. It wouldn't be as flawless as what she and her friends could make, but I knew she'd treasure the scarf just because I had made it for her.

We all began knitting in earnest. Even Sarah finished her burger and fries and pulled out the sweater she was making for her husband. Priscilla Carstairs said, "I began making small pieces when I was on stage. There might be an hour between when I was dressed and made-up and when I was called. I could have a small bag with me in the green room. A larger knitting bag was simply too cumbersome."

"How exciting," Clara said. "Were you an actress?"

We all looked at Priscilla, probably trying to trace the likeness to someone we might have seen on stage or screen. Priscilla smiled, somewhat condescendingly. "No, dear. I was a prima ballerina." She said the words slowly and with pride as though making sure even the deaf among us would know of her accomplishments.

Sarah sighed. "I always wanted to be a ballerina."

Priscilla laughed softly. "Every little girl wants to be a ballerina. Most don't have the discipline or the talent." She glanced at Sarah as though her gaze alone would make it clear that poor Sarah had neither. "I remember an early teacher of mine at Miss Adelaide's Dance School used to demonstrate my turnout for the rest of the class. Of course, to be a dancer, a girl needs extensive training as well as the right build. But what separates the prima ballerina from the girl in the back row of the corps de ballet is hard work. Discipline. Constant practice."

She shook her head. "Many a girl wishes to be a ballerina, but very few will see their dreams come true on stage."

Eileen looked at her, pausing with the pale blue cashmere wrapped around her finger. "I imagine there's also a certain ruthlessness involved, too, in getting to the top."

"Oh yes, indeed." Priscilla chuckled in a slightly evil way. "Oh, my goodness, yes. It may look like it's all tutus and bouquets of flowers, but it's the hard-hearted ones who survive. Good girls finish last."

We knitted on. Eileen told a story about little Henry waving his arms about when he saw his mother. Sarah talked about how well they were doing in marriage counseling and that her husband had promised to start helping with the dishes—if one of his favorite programs wasn't on TV. Since he seemed to be addicted to everything from the *EastEnders* to *Peaky Blinders* to *The Great British Bake Off,* I wasn't confident he'd be doing much dishwashing, but Sarah seemed hopeful and so I tried to be hopeful too.

I was counting stitches very carefully, determined I wasn't going to screw up this scarf. I wanted it to be as close to perfect as I could manage for my beloved grandmother. My shoulders were so tense from concentrating and probably holding my needles at the wrong angle that I was getting a pain between my shoulder blades. I didn't want to look uncomfortable in front of people who paid me for knitting supplies, so I glanced surreptitiously at my watch. Good. It was close enough to tea time that I could put down my work without creating suspicion that I wasn't tearing myself away from my favorite hobby.

I got up quietly and plugged in the kettle. I had teacups and saucers all ready, a silver mound of teaspoons and the tin of cookies along with a jug of milk and a sugar pot. I'd bought Christmas napkins too. I couldn't believe it when I discovered napkins that featured Christmas sweaters on them.

I fussed with the cups, putting a teaspoon on each saucer until the kettle boiled, then I made tea in the big Brown Betty. It needed a couple of minutes to brew, so I sat back down and picked up my knitting again. At least I'd been able to ease the kink between my shoulder blades.

I had the wool around my finger and I was just hooking it around the knitting needle, ready to knit a stitch, when the lights went out. There was no warning, no flickering. One minute I could see, and the next minute we were plunged into darkness.

CHAPTER 4

Someone gasped. It was so dark I couldn't see my knitting in front of me. In fact, I couldn't see anything at all. "What's going on?" Sarah, I thought, cried out.

"Don't worry," I said, with more confidence than I felt. "The power's gone out. It happened this afternoon. It will come back on again in a minute." I had no idea why I said that. It wasn't as though I had a secret line into the workings of whatever government department was in charge of lighting Oxford. However, I felt that since this was my shop, I should sound as though I were confident power would soon be restored. "In the meantime, I've got a flashlight and some candles somewhere."

The candles were my witch ones. I had been practicing lighting the wicks without the use of matches. However, I didn't think having candles spring magically to light while I recited a spell would soothe the already nervous knitters sitting here in the dark. I could hear shuffling and somebody coughing. Scrabbling noises, as, no doubt, women were

21

looking for their handbags so they could pull up the torch app on their smart phone.

Suddenly, there was an almighty crash and the sound of breaking china. Then someone screamed. An older woman. Joan? Priscilla? cried out, "I'm burning. Aaagh. I'm burning." One scream led, naturally, to another, as though there were a screaming virus and all the knitters succumbed.

"There's something on my feet. It's wet. I think it's blood!" This was Sarah.

"It's not blood," Hudson said in a soothing voice. "It's probably tea. You heard the crockery breaking."

I felt like screaming myself. It was like being in the middle of a horror movie. I was plunged back to the fears of childhood, thinking monsters were hiding under the bed, ready to pounce as soon as the lights went out. Only the lights *were* out, and it felt as though bad things were happening.

There were strange noises. Six panicked people's breathing sounded loud, and whoever was burned was definitely in distress, crying and moaning.

Naturally, I'd left my phone upstairs. I'd have to find my flashlight and some matches to light the candles with. I got up and felt my way to the wall. I bumped into someone and had to bite my lip to stop myself from screaming and running for where I thought the doorway might be.

The person I bumped into let out a startled cry, then said, "Is everyone all right?" It was Eileen's voice.

"No. I'm burned. I think the tea spilled on me," said Joan. I recognized her voice now that she wasn't screaming.

Oh, no. This was very bad. I flailed around in the dark until I felt the curtain. I was just pulling the fabric aside to go out into my front room where the candles were kept when suddenly the lights came back on.

It was almost as disorienting as when we'd been plunged into blackness.

I turned back to see that everyone was in their seats. Even Eileen was just sitting back down. The table was standing, but most of the cups and saucers had been knocked over, as had the teapot and kettle and the tin of cookies I'd made myself.

"That took me back to my childhood," Clara said, picking up her knitting once more. "Of course, that was before electricity."

Oh, perfect. There was Clara, now, doing the very thing I had warned her not to, reminiscing about a time far in the past. Luckily, Mabel was quicker-witted than I was. She laughed gaily. "You're not that old. I suppose next you'll tell us about how you used to play in the sand when the dinosaurs ruled the earth."

I heaved a sigh of relief. Nodded gratefully to Mabel. Clara looked somewhat abashed, returning busily to her sweater.

I surveyed the damage. About half the teacups were broken, but I had lots more upstairs. There was also another teapot, more milk and sugar. I even had extra cookies. "I can soon clear all this away," I said. "Do you all still want tea? It won't take a minute to make it again."

"I can help clear up," Hudson said, getting to his feet.

"I'll have tea and a biscuit," Sarah said, putting a hand to her chest. "I think I need it for the shock."

"Yes, tea would be lovely," Eileen agreed.

Joan held out her arm, and I could see her sweater dripping. "I've already had one cup thrown all over me. I'll drink the next one, thank you very much."

"I'm so sorry," I said instinctively. "Is it very bad?"

"Hurt like the devil at the time, but it's not too bad now."

"But how did the tea get knocked over?" Clara asked. "I didn't get up. Did one of you?"

We all looked at each other. No one said anything.

I glanced around, wondering why no one wanted to admit to knocking into the tea table. It wasn't as though they'd get in trouble. My gaze landed on Priscilla. Her head was bent forward, and her hands lay in her lap with her finished ornaments and the half-finished snowflake, but she wasn't crocheting.

As I looked at her, I got a very strange feeling. Whether it was my witch senses or my normal human ones, I wasn't sure, but the feeling was bad, as though something cold and slimy was balled in my chest. I took a step toward her. "Mrs. Carstairs?" Nothing. "Priscilla?"

She didn't react when I called her name the second time any more than she had the first.

I glanced around the knitting circle and found that everyone was staring at Priscilla Carstairs.

I went closer. I didn't want to touch her in case she'd fallen asleep. Maybe she was one of those people who could doze off the minute the lights were turned out. So as not to startle her, I squatted down onto my haunches at her feet so that I could look up into her face. I'd intended to call her name again, but the words got stuck in my throat.

A very strange sound came out of my mouth, sort of a hiccup, a gasp and a scream all rolled into one. Her eyes were open, and she appeared to be staring right down at me, but her gaze was glassy.

Her mouth was also open, and I could see a pair of black felt Santa boots just at the edge of her lower lip as though Santa had mistaken her throat for a chimney and dived down headfirst to deliver presents. I cried out, loudly this time, "Priscilla?"

Nothing.

I glanced around, and everyone in the room was staring at me now, looking as shocked as I felt. I didn't know what to do.

"What's happened?" Joan asked. "Has she fallen asleep? Has she had a fit?" She leaned forward. "Perhaps a stroke? Ask her to lift her arms above her head. That's a good way to tell if someone's had a stroke. Also, we must get her to speak and see if her speech is slurred." She paused. "There are other signs, but I can't remember them."

Hudson, who probably had an IQ in the millions, said, "That's right. FAST is the acronym. F for face. Is their face drooping on one side? A is for arms. Can the person lift both arms over their head? S is for speech. Is it slurred? And T is for Time. Which means, if those symptoms are present, it's time to call an ambulance."

I shook my head. "I don't think it's a stroke." I glanced around, looking up at them all from my crouched position. "She's got Santa stuck in her throat."

"What?" Hudson put down his knitting and came closer, as though having trouble believing me. And who could blame him? He bent his tall body way over to have a look, bending like a coat hanger. Eileen came and crouched beside me. The spilled tea had pooled around the chair legs, and a broken piece of china had landed in the middle of it, floating like a tiny boat.

"She's choking," Eileen said. "We must help her. Pull it out."

No one seemed anxious to put their hands into Priscilla Carstairs's mouth. Including me. However, it was my shop and my knitting circle, so apparently this was my problem.

Honestly, I'd rather have picked up live tarantulas, danced the tango with a cobra, kissed a toad ...

I reached forward. Gently, I tugged on Santa's boot, but nothing happened. The jolly red elf was completely stuck. I didn't think Priscilla was choking. I suspected we were already in the past tense, but I couldn't step away and not try to save this woman. I thought back to the first-aid course I'd taken in college. "Heimlich maneuver."

I barely remembered how to do it, but I should try. Hudson looked a lot stronger, and his height would help. Maybe he could do it. Then I saw Clara and Mabel exchange glances. Clara said, "I think it's a bit late for the Heimlich maneuver, dear." She shook her head. "There's no heartbeat. Her blood is not pumping."

Vampires have an incredible ability to smell out humans. Some of them are like sommeliers with fine wine—they can identify a human's blood type if they're close enough, so I wasn't surprised to discover that they could also sense whether the blood was pumping as it did in life or if the blood had stilled.

As it did in death.

CHAPTER 5

*S*till, I wanted to be sure. "Are you saying she's...?"

Clara nodded. "Dead." Then, as everyone was looking at her, obviously wondering how she could tell that from across the room, she said, "I was a nurse." *Please don't say in WWI.* "In—" Then, seeing my face, she said, "In a hospital. Death has an expression that is unmistakable." Then she said, in a funereal tone, "I'm so sorry." As though we were grieving family members.

"But that's impossible," Sarah said. "She was crocheting a beautiful white snowflake just minutes ago. Who dies in the middle of crocheting a snowflake?"

I had to agree. It didn't make sense.

Even though I believed Clara, I still reached for Priscilla's wrist and felt for a pulse. As I had feared, there wasn't one. It was creepy that her skin was still warm. A shudder went over me as I realized that this woman hadn't forced that Santa down her own throat. She'd been murdered right in front of me. Right in front of all of us.

Nyx was standing on the ground looking at the dead

woman. Eileen said, "I bet it was that cat. She probably thought those ornaments were cat toys."

Nyx looked at me, her golden eyes glowing. I knew how she felt. We always thought of witches being the only victims in witch trials, but their familiars had also been persecuted. I didn't like the way this conversation was going. "Nyx would never hurt anyone," I said. "Besides, are you suggesting that my cat forced a knitted toy down this woman's throat?" Okay, my cat was extremely special, but not that special.

"Well, Priscilla Carstairs didn't mistake her stuffed Santa for plum pudding, now, did she?" Eileen said.

Sarah's forehead crinkled. "If she'd choked on a knitted candy cane, it would've made more sense."

I straightened up to standing. "I'd better call the police."

"The police?" Eileen sounded alarmed. "But surely you should call an ambulance. A doctor. The woman was fine not ten minutes ago."

"The police will send an ambulance. But it's too late to revive her. I'm afraid Clara's right. Priscilla Carstairs is dead."

"But it was an accident. Must have been." She looked around at everyone in the room. "We were all here. It's not like anyone could sneak in and kill the woman. The lights were only out for a few minutes. We'd have heard the front door and known if a stranger had come among us. There's only one way in, through that curtain, and we would've known if anyone came in."

I didn't dare look at Clara and Mabel. There was another way in. And if a vampire had wanted to come among us, none of us humans would've been able to hear him. Or her.

But I didn't think a vampire had done this. Why would they?

And as I looked around from face to face, I realized that one of the people I was looking at was a killer.

There was a knock at the front door of the shop. We all startled and looked at each other. "That must be the police," Hudson said.

Clara glanced up from her knitting, and her nostrils twitched, but she didn't say anything. She and Mabel had gone back to stitching. Unlike everyone else in the room, death wasn't unfamiliar to them.

"That's impossible," Eileen said. "Lucy hasn't called them yet."

She had a point. The knock at my door was either a very late addition to the knitting circle or an ill-timed visitor. There was a third option. The way Clara and Mabel were looking pleased, I suspected I knew who was at the door.

"I'll see who's there, and I'll call the police," I said.

When I got to the front door, I wasn't a bit surprised to find Rafe Crosyer standing on the other side. He was tall, dark and pale. He looked like a combination of Mr. Rochester, Mr. Darcy, and Lord Byron with a hefty dose of Heathcliff thrown in. If he wasn't a vampire, Rafe would probably be the love of my life. Of course, if he wasn't a vampire, we'd never have met. When he'd been alive, Elizabeth was on the throne. The first one.

He didn't need me to open the door, locked or not. He was following social convention since he knew I had a knitting circle on tonight. When I'd opened the door, he stepped in and looked intently at my face. "What's going on? I was downstairs visiting your grandmother. I heard strange noises, and then I'm sure I smelled death." He touched my cheek. "You look pale."

I felt like snapping, "You should talk," but I knew he was being kind.

"One of the knitting circle died tonight." I gulped, voicing the unpleasant truth. "I think it was murder."

Rafe had pretty much seen, heard, and probably done everything in his half a millennium of existence, but even he looked confused. "A murder? What, you mean during the knitting circle?"

"It's ridiculous, I know." I was trying to keep my voice down, but I think my whisper was beginning to sound hysterical. "We had a power outage. One minute everyone was peacefully knitting, and the next—well, come and see for yourself."

He stopped me with a hand on my shoulder. "You mean you didn't see the perpetrator?"

"No. As I said, the lights went out. When they came back on, Priscilla Carstairs was dead."

"Priscilla Carstairs. Was she a very old woman?"

"Relatively old, I suppose. She was over eighty, I think."

"You're sure it wasn't natural causes?"

"Pretty sure."

His dark eyebrows rose at the sarcasm in my tone. "I'd better take a look."

While I was out there, I put in a call to Oxford CID. This wasn't the first time I'd ever called them about a murder, so I knew the drill. They asked the usual questions and said they would dispatch officers immediately. And, of course, no one was to leave or touch anything.

I entered the back room first, with Rafe following. He was an antiquarian book and manuscript expert who often advised the Bodleian Library and sometimes lectured at

Cardinal College. I suspected he'd had a client meeting, as he was wearing dark slacks, a black cashmere sweater and a houndstooth sports jacket. He looked like a very sexy university professor, except better dressed than most of them.

He had a commanding air about him, and as he walked in, everyone stopped talking and looked at him. I wasn't sure who knew him, so I said, "This is my friend Rafe Crosyer."

Eileen nodded to him. "Good evening, Rafe. You may not remember me, but you appraised my father's book collection a few years ago."

He smiled at her. "Of course I remember. He had some very fine volumes of Elizabethan poetry. But I believe the jewel in the collection was the first edition of Dr. Johnson's *Rasselas.*"

She looked delighted. "You do remember."

Joan Fawcett snapped, "We're not here for poetry. I don't know what he's doing in here, Lucy. A woman was killed, and this man just contaminated the scene."

I understood her irritation. She was busily dabbing at her sweater and skirt where the hot tea had spilled on her. "I must get home and get this burn seen to. My clothes have grown wet and clammy."

I really felt for her, but I reminded her that no one must leave before the police got there.

Hudson glanced at me, looking suddenly panicked. "How long will that be, then? I've got a paper to finish tonight."

I put my hands out. "Sorry. I have no idea. I called them, and they're on their way."

Rafe, meanwhile, had moved close to the dead woman. As I had done, he squatted on his haunches and looked up at her. "What a very odd way to kill someone," he said softly, almost to himself.

I stared at him, repressing the urge to giggle.

I understood what he meant, though. "Perhaps it was the closest thing to hand? And it was the right shape. Santa, with his big, round belly..." I didn't finish the sentence, but it was pretty clear where I was going. Santa had done the job of choking poor Priscilla Carstairs.

He nodded, and his gaze went to the ornaments still sitting on Priscilla Carstairs's lap from our show and tell. "I wonder why they chose the Santa."

CHAPTER 6

"But it was pitch-dark," I reminded Rafe. "Someone grabbed for a bauble. They wouldn't necessarily know which one they had hold of."

He rose and turned slowly, staring at each person in turn. I thought they each stopped breathing as he settled his cold gaze on them. If I'd killed someone, I was sure I'd tell everything if that chilly, commanding gaze fell on me. He'd have my confession out of me faster than a crochet hook can catch a stitch.

However, no one else in the room was as easily thrown off balance as I was, it seemed. Other than Sarah asking him if she had food on her blouse, all the crafters stayed silent as he surveyed them.

Rafe turned back to me. "Was it symbolic? Was there a message behind the use of Santa Claus as a murder weapon?"

Hudson nodded. He seemed to be treating this like an academic exercise in philosophy. "But Santa brings gifts. He doesn't kill people."

I voiced the thought I'd had earlier. "Priscilla Carstairs

was the only person here who was knitting things only for herself. Was that the message? That Christmas is a time for giving and thinking of others?"

"Pretty harsh way to deliver a message," Hudson said.

Eileen Crosby looked at Rafe as though considering his words. "Santa's fat."

Hudson stared at her. "Is this really the time to go into the dietary habits of Santa? Are you suggesting the jolly old elf should go on Weight Watchers? Quit sitting around all day making toys? Maybe start pumping some iron?" He pulled his fists up, demonstrating bicep curls.

"No. But Priscilla Carstairs was very rude to Sarah Lawson earlier." She turned her attention back to Rafe. "She made insensitive comments about her weight when Sarah ate a hamburger in front of us. I told her she was fat-shaming."

Clara nodded. "That's true. She did. It was most unkind."

Eileen looked at the victim of the fat-shaming. "Sarah? Did you make Priscilla Carstairs eat her words?"

There was a gasp. Then I realized it came from me. Talk about making the punishment fit the crime. Had Sarah made Priscilla choke on the rotund little Santa in the same way Priscilla had made her choke down that hamburger?

Sarah Lawson went bright red and then pale and started to rise from her chair and then sat back down again as though her legs wouldn't work. "Of course not. I would never. I don't even know how. I mean, why would someone die just from having a toy pushed in their mouth?"

I didn't know if she realized it, but she was making herself sound more guilty by the second. Perhaps she hadn't intended to kill Priscilla Carstairs; she'd only intended to teach her a lesson, and it had gone horribly wrong.

Rafe nodded. "The young lady's correct. Whoever did this held the nose as well. For an elderly woman, about two minutes without oxygen would likely cause death."

"How horrible," Eileen said. "But couldn't she have died of a heart attack?"

Rafe looked down at her where she was seated on the chair, little Henry's pale blue sweater forgotten on her lap. "If heart failure was caused by the attack, it's still murder. But that's for the police to determine."

He looked around. "I understand it was dark in here, but didn't you hear choking sounds?"

Joan made a sound like a snort. "No. What we heard was the crashing of crockery. Someone banged into that table and spilled boiling hot tea all over me. What everyone probably heard was my screams of agony."

"I'm so sorry that happened to you," I said soothingly. "Do you want me to take a look at your burns? I've got a first-aid kit in the shop."

In fact I had a very nice tea upstairs that I could make her. It was a witch's brew that would take away the pain and heal the burn quickly. However, I didn't really want to bring in supernatural medicine until the police had finished their very scientific investigation.

Based on the number of times I had been involved in murder investigations, I thought the police were already looking at me askance. Not that I'd ever committed any of the murders, but I felt I was already on thin ice with the local law enforcement authorities. The last thing I needed was for them to find out I was a witch.

I felt sorry for Joan Fawcett, but she was going to have to wait until the police were finished with us. Then I could make her my medicinal tea. In the meantime, all I could offer her was sympathy and drugstore remedies. Of course, if I had reason to want to avoid the police, Rafe and Clara and Mabel had even more. Witches at least were kind of trendy and could live openly in society. Why, my local coven organized events around our special days, like the recent Samhain potluck. Vampires, not so much.

There were broken dishes all over the floor, and the now cold tea had soaked into the area rug that I'd placed strategically over the trapdoor that led down to the tunnels. I itched to get my broom and mop and clean up the mess, but I knew I couldn't. Not until the police had finished their investigation.

So we sat there. One by one, the crafters resumed their knitting or crochet. At least it gave them something to do. I couldn't concentrate though.

Nyx, naturally, had to go and investigate. She didn't go near Priscilla Carstairs. I think that she could also smell something off. But she made her way over to the broken dishes. The milk jug had smashed, and there was a puddle of spilled milk on the floor that had mingled with the spilled sugar and made a sticky mess. Nyx looked at it for a long moment, and I thought she might lap it up, but she wasn't much for milk. She preferred her high-end tuna out of her own special dish upstairs.

When she'd finished investigating, she looked at me, I thought, with pity that I was in yet another murderous pickle and then pushed her way through the curtained doorway.

Rafe made a slight motion with his chin toward the front of the shop, and I assumed that meant he wanted to talk to me away from the knitting circle. I excused myself, saying I thought I heard the police at the door, even though I'd heard no such thing. I glanced back as I left and saw everyone knitting or crocheting busily. Were it not that Priscilla Carstairs's hands were unnaturally still and her acid tongue unnaturally silent, it would've just been another typical night in my knitting circle.

In fact, it was so much like a regular knitting circle that I thought Clara had forgotten once again that she was among humans. Her knitting speed had increased to the point that anyone attempting to watch her would grow dizzy. As we passed her, I gave her a warning squeeze on the shoulder. She looked up at me puzzled, and so I leaned down and whispered as softly as I could, "Slow down with the needles."

She looked stricken. "Oh, I forgot. Sorry."

I could only hope that she would remember to knit at human speed and that the mortals were so rattled at being in the company of the dead woman that they'd believe their eyes were playing tricks on them.

CHAPTER 7

*R*afe followed me out into the shop. Nyx was about to jump up into her usual spot in the window, but when she saw me she instead made her way to the connecting door that led upstairs to our flat. I completely understood her desire to get away from this and only wished I could follow her. I opened the door for her, and she wasted no time getting out of Dodge.

I asked Rafe the question that had been bothering me ever since the lights came on after the blackout and I realized that one of our number was dead. "Rafe, I locked the trapdoor, but is there any way one of the vampires could have come up when the lights were out?"

He looked down his nose at me as though offended I would think his vampires had so little power. "Your flimsy lock wouldn't keep one of us out. But we all knew it was your knitting circle night, so I can assure you that none of us even attempted to come up that way."

Well, that was what I'd thought, but it was still a relief. "Then I don't understand. I locked the front door, and I'd have heard if anyone had come in. That means that someone in that contented little knitting circle is a killer."

"Yes, I think that is the obvious conclusion."

"But who? And why?" Two excellent questions, if I did say so myself.

"Can you think of any reason why anyone in that knitting circle would've wanted that woman dead?"

"No. Sarah Lawson really did look mortified when Priscilla fat-shamed her for eating a hamburger and french fries, but that's about it."

Rafe's sensitive nostrils flared. "Fast food is an abomination to the senses."

I thought someone who drank blood for breakfast, lunch and dinner wasn't really in a position to judge. "And Eileen was offended when she said her beloved grandson had a brain the size of a tadpole."

Rafe looked quite interested. "Does he?"

"He's about a month old. Probably."

I thought of them all in there, still knitting. "Would it take much strength to kill her?"

He considered my question. "I shouldn't think so. She was old, not expecting an attack. I should think anyone in that room could've done it."

I was surprised. "Even Joan Fawcett?"

"Which one is she?"

"She's the other old lady. The one who was burned by the tea."

"Yes, if she was motivated enough, I should think she could."

"But the strongest one in the room had to be Hudson."

"Any reason he might want her dead?"

"He seems nice enough. He and Sarah Lawson are quite friendly. Could it have been a chivalrous act?"

One of Rafe's eyebrows went up. "If so, then that young man needs lessons on chivalry."

I leaned back against a wall of wool, which had a comforting feeling, as though the wall was giving me a hug. "Could the murder have been premeditated?"

He shook his head. "The power went out on the whole block. It was caused by the windstorm. No one could have planned that."

"So it was definitely a crime of opportunity."

"I would say so. Possibly the murderer had planned to take Priscilla Carstairs's life this evening and had another method in mind." He began to pace. "But then why not use it? Why take such a risk? The lights could've gone on at any moment. No, I believe it was done on impulse. Think, Lucy. Priscilla Carstairs must've said or done something this evening that caused her murderer to rise up."

I felt helpless. "It was only the usual chitchat that relative strangers share with each other."

"I don't like to leave you, but Clara and Mabel will keep you safe. Unfortunately, they'll be forced to stay for the police investigation."

I hadn't thought about how awkward it could be if Clara pulled out her birth certificate that said she was more than a hundred and fifty years old. "Will they pass?"

"Oh yes. All of us have valid identification. However, since I wasn't part of the knitting circle, I should leave before the police arrive. But do call me if I can do anything."

"You can put your exceedingly large brain to work on trying to figure out who killed Priscilla Carstairs and why."

He nodded. "I'll find out everything I can about her. What do you know?"

"What do I know about Priscilla Carstairs?" I thought about the dead woman. "She was an excellent knitter. She'd been a prima ballerina, or so she said. She was very proud of her dance career. She'd been coming to the knitting circle because she was widowed."

"Any children?"

"No. She said it wasn't compatible with a dancing career. She was the only person who was knitting things for herself. Everyone else was knitting holiday gifts." It suddenly struck me how sad that was. "Imagine having no one who would want your beautiful knitted garments."

He made a rude noise. "There are plenty of charities that would be only too happy to have warm items to give to the homeless and the destitute."

I knew he was right. The vampire knitting club turned out enough knitted hats and socks and sweaters and blankets to keep most of Oxfordshire warm throughout the winter. They donated a lot of their hand-knitted goods to charity.

"So we know she wasn't charitable. She was thoughtless of other people's feelings, and she seemed very selfish. She even admitted to having a ruthless streak back when she was a ballerina."

"That's quite a bit to go on. I'll start doing some research. Meanwhile, I'll keep my phone on. If you need me to check anything else or you just need me—" He looked me intently. "You can call me anytime."

He wasn't just saying those words. I knew he meant them. And as much as I wanted him to stay, I also knew he was right to leave before the police arrived. He and Detective Inspector

Ian Chisholm didn't always see eye to eye. I suspected the fact that I'd briefly dated Ian had something to do with it.

Rafe tilted his head to one side. "I can hear the police cars. They're on their way." He touched my shoulder. "I'll come and see you when they've left."

He slipped out the front door, and I locked it behind him. Not that I was too worried about dangers from outside, not when it seemed I had a murderer on the inside.

Safety in numbers, I reminded myself.

So long as the lights stayed on.

I went to fetch the first-aid kit, the one that had no magic ingredients whatsoever, and took it into the back room.

As I walked in, I realized that I knew who had killed Priscilla Carstairs.

I just didn't know how to prove it.

CHAPTER 8

I retreated back to the shop and then quickly ran upstairs to my flat and picked up my phone. I could hear the police cars pulling up as I rapidly texted Rafe, asking him to check two pieces of information for me.

Then, slipping my phone into my pocket, I returned downstairs.

I opened the shop door to the two detectives who were standing there. Detective Inspector Ian Chisholm gave me a baleful look—and who could blame him? This was not the first time he'd been called to my shop because of a dead body on the premises. I was beginning to think the shop was cursed. Again, not for the first time.

As soon as this was over, I was going to ask the witches in my family who were more powerful than I to come by for yet another cleansing.

Ian probably didn't believe in curses, but I was sure even his rational mind boggled at being here again because of a suspicious death.

He didn't waste any time on chitchat. "This is Sergeant

Barnes." I nodded to the redheaded man. "Tell us what happened."

I did, as best I could, explaining about the knitting circle and the suspicious death. Ian's gaze never left my face, but I tried not to let it unnerve me and to explain the facts as succinctly as I could.

He stopped me halfway through my recital. "Wait. Perhaps we'd better see for ourselves."

The paramedics came in right behind him. He signaled them to wait, and he and Sergeant Barnes went ahead and into the back room. All the knitters were in exactly the places where I had left them. There was low-voiced conversation that stopped as we entered.

Ian looked all around the circle once and then twice before even identifying which was the dead woman.

He called in the paramedics, who came in with a medical kit. I was surprised he didn't ask us all to leave the room, but he didn't. So we sat and watched as a doctor examined Priscilla.

Weirdly, I waited anxiously for the verdict, even though I was positive there was no life left in Priscilla Carstairs. Sure enough, after a short examination, the doctor looked up at Ian and shook her head. Then I finally accepted that Priscilla Carstairs was dead. Murdered during a knitting circle.

Now, Ian asked us all to move into the front part of the shop. The police photographer arrived with the forensics team, who greeted me by name. Honestly, you know you've been involved in too many deaths when the forensic people know your name.

The photographer brought in strong lights, and with the light and sounds of activity coming from behind the curtain, it was as though they were making a movie back there. I only wished that were true.

We stood around awkwardly among the walls of wool and table of Christmas knitting displays. "I don't want to take you all down to the station."

Hudson said in a panicked tone, "No. I have a paper due in the morning. I've got to get home to finish it."

Ian looked at me, and I could practically read his thoughts. He was contemplating asking me if everyone could go upstairs to my flat. The only problem with that idea was that I would be hosting a murderer in my home. However, since I'd already had that person in my back room all evening, I didn't think I had a lot more to risk. "I'm willing to have everyone come upstairs to my flat if you'd like."

He looked grateful and relieved and at the same time worried. But since it was the most practical solution, he agreed. I opened the door leading up to my flat, and the knitters headed up that way. Ian held me back with a hand on my arm. "Thank you, Lucy. I'll keep you safe. If necessary, I'll have an officer assigned to protect you until we have the perpetrator in custody."

I appreciated his concern for me. In fact, I appreciated a lot of things about Ian Chisholm. In some ways, he was the light to Rafe's darkness. Still, our brief dating experience hadn't turned out that well. Not that it was entirely his fault—he'd been the victim of a love potion gone wrong. But, even so, I couldn't change history. Much as I might like to.

Hudson was helping Joan Fawcett into the most comfortable chair when I got to the top of the stairs with Ian Chisholm. My lounge wasn't terribly big, and there wasn't enough seating for all of us, so I went to the dining room and fetched some more chairs. As people began to settle them-selves, Ian said, "I want you all to sit in exactly the same order as you were downstairs."

I looked around, and strangely, we had instinctively done that. I moved my wooden chair beside Sarah Lawson. And then, with a heavy heart, placed an empty chair where Priscilla Carstairs would have been, between Eileen and Joan.

Ian sat just outside our circle, and Sergeant Barnes stood with his notebook open at the top of the stairway. I strongly suspected that there were more officers downstairs should the killer try to make a break for it.

Ian began. "Normally, I would interview each of you sepa-rately, but due to the peculiar nature of Priscilla Carstairs's death, I'm going talk to you all at once. I want each of you to listen to the other person's interview and let me know if you hear inconsistencies or have anything to add. Try to remember everything that happened, in the order it happened."

He didn't say that one of us was a killer, but I think we all realized that by now. These were nice people I'd knitted with, sold wool and magazines to. I hated to think of them harboring violence while they'd browsed through my wools, but it must be true. He looked around at us all. "This is where you were sitting?"

We all nodded.

He started by getting each of us to go through the evening as we remembered it. He began with Sarah Lawson. She looked nervous, and her color was up. She talked about bringing in her hamburger and how mean Priscilla had been to her. But then she assured him that even though she'd been hurt by the dead woman's unfeeling remarks, she wouldn't kill anyone.

"And did you know Mrs. Carstairs before tonight?"

She looked around at all of us helplessly. "Well, yes, of course. We've all been coming to this knitting circle for several weeks. It's not always the same people, but I've knitted with Priscilla Carstairs on several occasions."

"And before that? Did you know her?"

"No. We never met." She made a face. "Once this knitting circle was over, I would've been perfectly happy never to see her again."

It was probably a stupid thing to admit to the police, but on the other hand, her honest admission made her sound more innocent.

I asked if Ian would mind if I took care of Joan Fawcett's burn, as I was still lugging the first-aid kit around and hadn't had a chance to treat her scald. He said that was fine. I moved closer to Joan and opened my first-aid kit.

Ian asked Sarah Lawson exactly what she'd experienced when the lights went out. "Take your time and be as specific as you can."

She took a moment and closed her eyes before beginning. "It was a shock. One minute I was counting stitches on my needle, and the next minute everything was dark. I heard rustling and maybe someone said, 'What's going on?' I can't really remember. Next thing, I heard a crash and the sound of breaking china. Someone screamed. And then Lucy was telling us not to worry, that she had candles somewhere."

"And then?"

"And then the lights went back on. It took a few minutes before we even realized Priscilla Carstairs was dead."

CHAPTER 9

"When the lights went back on, was everyone in the same spot as before the power cut?"

"Um." She closed her eyes again and left them closed as though a movie was playing on the back of her eyelids. "Lucy was standing up. Otherwise, I think everyone was sitting in the same spot."

Ian moved on to Hudson next and got pretty much the same story, though Hudson was able to add more detail. He remembered me and Eileen bumping into each other, and he remembered more of what I'd said. While they were talking, I helped Joan take off her sweater, and I smoothed a topical ointment on the red skin where the hot tea had scalded her left arm. It wasn't blistered, so I didn't think there would be any permanent damage. I didn't want to think of her skin burning in the aftermath of having scalding tea dumped all over it and decided I would make her a cup of my special healing tea after all.

I went to the kitchen and put the kettle on to boil. I listened with half an ear as Hudson said he hadn't known the victim before knitting circle began and he hadn't noticed anything strange during the blackout. "Though I did hear something odd. The two older ladies sitting beside me were talking to themselves. They said something about blackouts during the war. I didn't know what war?"

I turned to stare. Clara and Mabel looked guilty. Again. I made a silent vow to ban them from all human knitting circles from now on. Finally, Clara said, "I was talking about my mother. She used to tell stories about the war."

In a hurry to get back out there, I brewed my special tea and, circling my hand over the cup, quietly muttered,

Let this tea soothing be to one who suffers burning pain.
Take away the sting and let healthy skin remain.
So I wish, so mote it be.

I took the mug into the lounge and offered it to Joan. I didn't offer anyone else a drink, and no one even seemed to notice. Or perhaps the very thought of tea made them feel bilious.

I resumed my seat. Ian interviewed Mabel next, and I tried to refrain from clenching every muscle in my body with dread. Please let her not tell him things that no human should know, like how she'd actually heard Priscilla's blood stop pumping and how she'd smelled death. But fortunately, Mabel had the sense to repeat nearly word for word what Sarah and Hudson had said. Clara did the same.

Eileen was next, and as Ian turned his attention to her, I think we were all aware of the empty chair next to her.

"You were sitting beside Mrs. Carstairs. I want you to

think very carefully about what you saw or felt and what you did, during and after the blackout."

She shrugged her shoulders and looked around the room as though we might all be able to help her out. "I was busy knitting my little grandson a sweater. Because it's so tiny, it's very important to get everything right. It's got a cable pattern, you see, and I was counting, making certain that I had all my stitches in the correct order when the lights went out. I admit the first thing I felt was irritation because I had just worked out exactly where I was in the pattern and now I was going to lose my place."

"You weren't frightened or startled?"

"Not really. It was only a power cut."

"Did you hear anything from the victim?"

"I think she made a sound as though she were annoyed. She muttered something. 'This is nice,' you know, in a sarcastic way. I heard rustling like in the theater before the movie starts when the lights go down. Suddenly you're aware of other people shuffling and sighing and coughing and so on. Then I heard the crash of dishes and things breaking. Joan screamed, and I wasn't certain what to do. I wanted to get up and help her, but it was so dark, I was afraid of slipping or hurting myself on something that was broken.

I heard Lucy say that she would find some candles, and then I thought I'd better get up to see if I could help Joan. I suppose in the darkness, Lucy and I became disoriented, and we collided with each other. Then, shortly after that, the power went back on. I think in the relief of having our vision restored, none of us realized that poor Priscilla was dead."

She swallowed, and I saw the shudder go over her skin. "It was horrible."

As he'd asked all the others, Ian asked her if she had known the victim before the knitting circle began to meet. She hesitated for a long time. The moment stretched too long, until I suppose even she realized that if she pretended now that she didn't know the woman, none of us would believe it, including the police. "Yes. I did. It was on a professional matter. I really shouldn't say more."

Ian looked at her, and when he put on his tough cop face, he could be quite intimidating. "I can take you down to the station and interview you in a private room, if that would make you more comfortable. Please remember, this is a criminal investigation."

Eileen looked at the empty chair as though she might get Priscilla's permission to go on and, receiving none, said, "I don't suppose it matters too much now that the poor woman is dead. We represented her husband in their divorce." She hesitated, then added, "If everything he claimed was true, she wasn't very nice to him."

"Divorce?" Sarah asked her. "I thought she said she was widowed."

"She was divorced from the man first. I think she called herself a widow as it made her sound like the victim."

"Did you feel someone walk behind you before they knocked into the table and broke all that crockery?"

"No. I didn't."

"You and Lucy bumped into each other. You're the only person who seems to have been on their feet during the blackout. Are you sure it wasn't you who caused the accident with the table?"

I discovered that Eileen had a steely glare just as tough as Ian's. It was impressive. "I'm very sure."

They stared at each other for about thirty seconds in a standoff that I knew I'd have lost in the first microsecond.

He turned, finally, to Joan Fawcett. He asked her the same questions he'd asked everyone else. She said very much what the rest of them had. When the lights went out, she'd heard some shuffling. Someone coughed. And she looked at Eileen. "And yes, I did hear Priscilla mutter something. I was wondering whether I should put my crochet away when I was hit by scalding tea. Well, I didn't understand it was tea at the time. All I knew was the shock of great pain. I'm afraid I screamed. After that, I was so completely taken up with mopping myself up that I didn't notice anything else."

"Did you hear anyone behind you?"

"Now you mention it, I did. I heard footsteps and then the impact as someone hit that table and then, as I said, I was hit by the burning tea and also heard all the china breaking on the floor."

He looked at her. "This is very important, Mrs. Fawcett. Do you have any idea who that person was who knocked into the table?"

"I think it might've been Sarah Lawson."

CHAPTER 10

Sarah sat up straight and shrieked, "What?"

Joan shrugged helplessly. "It was a heavy-footed person. That's all I know. And, of course, Priscilla had been very unkind to Sarah." She let her words hang in the air, which they did, like a fog or a bad smell.

I felt the vibration that told me a text message was coming in. To my relief, it was from Rafe. He'd worked very quickly, and I had the answers to both my questions. It wasn't proof, but his new information confirmed what I already believed.

I put my phone back in my pocket as Ian asked, almost by rote now, "And Mrs. Fawcett, did you know the victim before this evening?"

"Yes, like everyone else, I saw her most weeks at the knitting circle."

He nodded. "And you'd never seen her before?"

She shook her head. "No. Never."

I didn't like what I had to do, but Joan Fawcett had just told a lie. "Are you sure?" I asked her.

Everyone turned to me, looking startled. I wasn't supposed to be the one asking the questions, but Ian Chisholm knew that I had a bad habit of getting involved in murders. I didn't like to boast, but I had actually helped solve a couple of them. And I felt certain I was on my way to solving this one.

Joan turned to me in surprise. "What can you mean, Lucy? I suppose I might have seen the woman in your knitting shop, but I didn't pay any attention."

I glanced at Ian, and he gave an imperceptible nod for me to go on. I knew I had to be very careful here or I'd make a mess of things. "Didn't you once attend Miss Adelaide's Ballet School?"

She looked stunned for a moment, and I saw her mouth open as she went slack-jawed. Then she shut her mouth so hard, her false teeth snapped together with a clatter. "My goodness, that was donkey's years ago. But yes, I took dance lessons when I was young."

Hudson glanced over now, looking interested. "Miss Adelaide's Ballet School? Wasn't that the school that Priscilla Carstairs said she'd attended?" He looked around at us all. "She was just telling the story tonight."

Eileen furrowed her brow and then nodded. "Yes, Hudson, I believe you're right."

Joan Fawcett shifted in her seat, finding a more comfortable position. "I should think a great number of girls attended Miss Adelaide's Ballet School. It was famous. She turned out a number of dancers who went on to great careers."

"Yes," I said. "But you and Priscilla Carstairs were exactly the same age." And thank you, Rafe for that information. "You must have been there at the same time."

She shrugged irritably, looking at Ian now. "Even if we were, I could hardly be expected to remember something that happened nearly seventy years ago."

I let a beat of silence pass. If there was one thing I'd learned in my brief time of interrogating people, it was the importance of silence. Letting that pause build until the suspect was uncomfortably waiting for the next question. I let her wait, and the silence grew in the room. Ian didn't say anything. He let me have the floor. "You said to Eileen that you didn't suffer from rheumatism. That you walk with a cane because you had an accident when you were young. What was that accident?"

I'd deliberately tried to throw her off with a question she hadn't expected. She began to look offended and sat up ramrod straight. The cameo brooch at her throat caught the light from the lamps. She put down her tea with a snap. "I really don't think that's any of your business."

I looked at Ian. We weren't doing good cop/bad cop so much as real cop/fake cop, but he'd obviously decided to trust me in this unorthodox investigation. He said, "If Lucy thinks your injury could have a bearing on this case, then I must ask you to answer the question. Again, if you're uncomfortable speaking in front of the group, we can take you down to the station and ask you questions there."

She appealed to the room at large, holding her hands out. "This is ridiculous. I suffered a fall. My leg was broken in several places and never healed properly. It happened years go."

Ian cut his gaze to me, and I knew he was giving me silent

permission to continue. I appreciated his trust in me and very much hoped I didn't screw this up. "But where did you fall, Joan?" I felt sad pushing her, this old lady who'd suffered for so many years. "And what did you fall off?"

There was a terrible silence. She looked at me, and whatever she saw must have told her I'd guessed the truth.

And then her face seemed to fall in on itself. "How did you know?" she asked me. "How could you possibly know?"

It was like there were only two of us in the room now. "Because you were the only one who was burned with the tea. From where the table was located, if the tea hit you on your left arm, it should've hit Priscilla and possibly Eileen. But no one was scalded but you."

"But Sarah could've done it, anyone could, and they could have picked up the teapot and knocked it over so it splashed on me."

"But that's not what happened, is it? Are you really going to let Sarah take the blame for this?"

She picked up her cold tea and took a sip. Her hands were shaking when she put the cup back down. "No. You're right."

"Priscilla Carstairs wasn't killed because of something that happened tonight. It happened many years ago. Why don't you tell us what happened? All those years ago?"

CHAPTER 11

*H*er eyes were clouded with age, and she gazed across the room as though she were gazing across the decades. Into the past.

"You guessed it, of course. Priscilla and I both attended Miss Adelaide's Ballet School. We were about twelve when we met, and we were the two best students in the class." She smiled a little. "Priscilla was right. Miss Adelaide loved to show the rest of the class her turnout. It was excellent. But I was the more graceful dancer.

"Miss Adelaide herself gave us both extra coaching. We were her star pupils, and she promised us that with hard work and dedication we could end up as professional dancers. Both of us shared the dream and worked tirelessly. We pushed each other on, but I thought it was healthy competition."

"But something happened," I said.

She nodded. She looked relieved to finally be telling the story. "We reached the age of seventeen and both had the opportunity to audition for a coveted spot as a junior dancer in a prestigious dance company.

"I can't tell you the excitement I felt. There were lots of girls there, but it very soon became clear that Priscilla and I were in competition for one of those coveted spots. We'd been practicing at the barre in the rehearsal hall to warm up for the final audition, and then Priscilla suggested that we go to the stage and see what it looked like. We'd just take a peek, she said, and then we'd run back and get ready for our final audition.

"She'd always been so jealous of me that I should have been suspicious that she suddenly became so friendly." Joan sighed heavily. "But I was a fool. I went with her. There we were, two young ladies in our black leotards with our hair done up in tight buns, dance slippers on our feet. We practiced arabesque and did some leaps across the stage. And then Priscilla walked to the very edge of the stage and looked over. "Come over here and look. That's where the orchestra will play for us when we're both famous ballerinas."

There was complete silence in the room. No one even breathed.

"I followed her to the edge of the stage, and when I leaned over to look into the orchestra pit, Priscilla pushed me off the stage."

Even though her story had led us here, I still felt my heart jump. Sarah gasped.

"I don't to this day know what she'd intended, but I knew the minute I hit the ground that something terrible had happened. I heard my leg break. I lost consciousness, and when I woke up, I was in the hospital."

"Oh, how awful," Eileen said.

"Priscilla got the place, of course. I told my parents what had happened, and they complained to the ballet company and to Miss Adelaide. Priscilla, naturally, claimed that going on the stage had been my idea and while looking over into the orchestra pit, I had slipped and fallen. We were friends, she kept saying. And, naturally, anyone who'd seen us at the audition had witnessed nothing but friendly behavior."

Her hands tightened into fists. Her skin was so thin, I could see the white bones of her knuckles. "She even came to see me in hospital. Brought me flowers and pretended she believed her own lies. I screamed at her. Told her if I ever saw her again, I would kill her."

Clearly, Joan was a woman of her word.

"To give the ballet company credit, they didn't take her on after all. No doubt they weren't sure who to believe but didn't want to take the chance on a girl who might have harmed a rival dancer. That didn't stop Priscilla. She kept auditioning, and eventually she was taken in by a ballet company. I followed her career for a while. Every promotion, every triumph felt as though she'd pushed me off the stage once more. It was too painful, and eventually I stopped."

She sighed. "It had been so long, I didn't think I even hated her anymore. Then, when this thin old woman turned up at the knitting circle, I didn't even recognize her. It had been sixty-five years, so she didn't look like her younger self, and she had a different surname. It wasn't until she told that story tonight about Miss Adelaide's school and I really looked at her that I recognized her. She was the same Priscilla who had destroyed my career and left me a virtual cripple for all my life while she went on to stardom. She got away with it for so long. And when she spoke to Sarah that way, I knew she was still cruel."

"Did you intend to kill her?" I asked.

"I don't know. I was filled with hatred. It was as fresh as the day she killed my dance career. When the lights went out, I simply acted. I reached out blindly for one of those stupid baubles that she was knitting for herself. I don't think I intended to kill her. I just wanted to shove her appalling selfishness and cruelty down her throat. But then she started making noises, and so I had to knock the table to create enough noise to cover it. I began to scream that I'd been burned and then caught the teapot before it fell, spilled some onto myself, and then dropped that on the floor as well."

She shrugged. "Then I sat back down in my seat and waited for the lights to come back on. I didn't know whether Priscilla was dead or alive, and I didn't much care either way. It was how she must have felt when she pushed me off that stage."

Ian nodded to the sergeant, who formally arrested Joan Fawcett, and then she was led away, leaning heavily on her cane. As she passed me, she said, "Thank you for the tea. I feel much better. Even the pain in my leg is better."

I'd felt it was the least I could do when I'd known I was going to turn her in to Ian. "I'll make sure to send you some," I promised her. Even if I had to deliver it to jail.

After she left, we all sat there, stunned, until Ian said, "You're all free to go. Just make sure you leave your contact details with the constable downstairs. We may need to contact you again."

Hudson got up and gathered his things, then turned to

me. "I'm sorry, Lucy. But I don't think I'll be coming to knitting circle anymore."

Eileen packed up little Henry's sweater and pushed it back into her knitting bag. "I don't think I'll be back, either."

Sarah Lawson opened her mouth to speak, and I held up my hands. "Don't worry. Knitting circle is canceled until further notice."

Mabel and Clara left with the others, and I suspected they'd soon tell the other vampires what had happened.

After they left, only Ian remained. "You handled that well. How did you know about Joan Fawcett and Priscilla Carstairs's past?"

"Some of it was from scraps of conversation I picked up, and some was just a lucky guess." And I couldn't tell him about my secret accomplice. The vampire who was at this moment downstairs on a very powerful computer, no doubt waiting for Ian to leave.

"Well, I'm sorry your evening had to end this way." His gaze went to my kitchen. "But I'll have one of those biscuits if I may. They look delicious."

I sent him away with a bag of half a dozen white chocolate and cranberry cookies.

Soon I'd have to go downstairs and clean up the mess, but not quite yet.

I sat on my couch, and Nyx came out of the bedroom, making sure everyone was gone before she jumped up and settled onto my lap.

"Nyx," I said, "I'm not sure knitting circle for humans was such a good idea."

She rubbed her head against my arm, which was her way of asking for a belly rub. I heard the downstairs door open and light footsteps coming up the stairs. "Oh, Lucy, Rafe and Mabel and Clara have been telling us all about your ordeal. What a dreadful evening."

It was my grandmother. She might be undead, but she was still my beloved gran. She sat down beside me to give me a hug. Behind her came Rafe. "We saw Joan Fawcett being led away. Did you get her to confess?"

"I did."

"Well done, Lucy."

"I couldn't have done it without you researching Miss Adelaide's Ballet School and Priscilla's career."

Gran said, "You two make a very good team."

And then she pulled out her knitting. "I've invited a few of the others to come up. I thought we'd have an impromptu knitting circle of our own. Just to make you feel better."

"Thanks, Gran." She must have known I didn't feel like being alone right now. I felt bad that I couldn't work on her Christmas gift, but the truth was, I didn't feel much like knitting, either.

Theodore and Sylvia arrived next with Clara and Mabel. They were whispering and looking pleased with themselves. Gran said, "We have a surprise for you. To cheer you up."

Theodore passed me a gift bag, looking bashful. "It's from all of us. A little gift for you to wear in the shop."

The vampires often gave me things to wear, but I could tell from their expressions that this was something special. I pulled out the knitted sweater and immediately felt my spirits lift.

It was a Christmas jumper. Possibly one of the most ridiculous sweaters ever knit by man or vampire.

It was red, with a large green Christmas tree featured on

the front, with a big gold star on top stitched in actual gold thread, and on the tree were hand-knitted baubles that hung off the sweater. I could tell Nyx thought it was an elaborate cat toy, and when her paw headed to one of the swinging, sparkling balls, I stopped her. "Don't even think about it."

"Try it on," Mabel said.

I didn't need more encouragement. I pulled the sweater on over my black T-shirt and pulled my hair out of the neck. The sweater was a perfect fit, of course. I ran to the mirror and admired myself, turning this way and that. Every time I moved, the Christmas ornaments danced.

"It's beautiful," I said. "I love it. I can't wait to wear it in the shop."

And I decided that I would never mock the tradition of the Christmas jumper again.

Thanks for reading *Cat's Paws and Curses*. I hope you'll consider leaving a review, it really helps.

Read on for a sneak peek of *Gingerdead House,* the Holiday Whodunnit in *The Great Witches Baking Show* series.

Gingerdead House, Chapter I

ONE OF THE things that happens when you take part in the Great British Baking Contest, a reality baking show that's taken the world by storm, is that you become a celebrity.

Maybe that's not completely true if you get sent home in the first couple of weeks, but as you make it towards the end of the contest and there are only a few bakers left, then people get behind you like you're a favorite football or basketball team.

At least that was my experience as a contestant on the beloved show.

This meant that as December got closer, we amateur bakers all had plenty of invitations to appear in public, most of them for something charitable. And how do you turn down a charity at Christmas?

The show's producers recommended that each of us chose one, at the most two public charity events to support, so we didn't get spread thinner than the butter on a dieter's sandwich. Also, they were absolutely clear that none of these extra-curricular events were sanctioned by the production company or in any way affiliated with it.

What was great about that was we weren't being judged, our creations weren't scrutinized, and there was no danger of being sent home. What a relief!

The event I chose to support was a gingerbread house baking and decorating contest in Bath. The event was raising money for the local city farm that encouraged eating local produce and introduced children to urban farming, among other events.

A number of local celebrities had been invited to make and decorate a gingerbread house. We would do the building and decorating at Bath's famous assembly rooms over a November weekend during the Christmas market, which drew some three hundred thousand visitors. People would vote for their favorites. Each vote cost money that would be donated to the city farm. Since I was a baking contestant, I liked the idea of a charity related to food.

The nice thing about baking a gingerbread house is that it's relatively easy. Yes, if this was part of the televised baking contest, I'd be expected to add strange ingredients and go to outrageous lengths to impress two very critical judges. But in a fun charity event, where I'd be judged not on the flavor or consistency of the gingerbread, but the overall style and decoration of the house, I could keep my recipe simple and put all my efforts into the house and its decoration. This was an amazing relief to me.

Order your copy of *Gingerdead House* today or keep reading for a sneak peek of book 1 in *The Great Witches Baking Show* series.

A Note from Nancy

Dear Reader,

Thank you for reading my *Vampire Knitting Club* Holiday Whodunnit. I am so grateful for all the enthusiasm this series has received. I have plenty more stories about Lucy and her undead knitters planned for the future.

I hope you'll consider leaving a review and please tell your friends who like cozy mysteries.

Review *Cat's Paws and Curses* on Amazon, Goodreads or BookBub. It makes such a difference.

Your support is the wool that helps me knit up these yarns.

Join my newsletter for a free prequel, *Tangles and Treasons*, the exciting tale of how the gorgeous Rafe Crosyer was turned into a vampire.

I hope to see you in my private Facebook Group. It's a lot of fun. www.facebook.com/groups/NancyWarrenKnitwits

Turn the page for a sneak peek of *The Great Witches Baking Show* (book 1 in the series).

Until next time,
Happy Reading,
Nancy

THE GREAT WITCHES BAKING SHOW

Excerpt from Prologue

Elspeth Peach could not have conjured a more beautiful day. Broomewode Hall glowed in the spring sunshine. The golden Cotswolds stone manor house was a Georgian masterpiece, and its symmetrical windows winked at her as though it knew her secrets and promised to keep them. Green lawns stretched their arms wide, and an ornamental lake seemed to welcome the swans floating serene and elegant on its surface.

But if she shifted her gaze just an inch to the left, the sense of peace and tranquility broke into a million pieces. Trucks and trailers had invaded the grounds, large tents were already in place, and she could see electricians and carpenters and painters at work on the twelve cooking stations. As the star judge of the wildly popular TV series *The Great British Baking Contest,* Elspeth Peach liked to cast her discerning eye over the setup to make sure that everything was perfect.

When the reality show became a hit, Elspeth Peach had been rocketed to a household name. She'd have been just as happy to be left alone in relative obscurity, writing cookbooks and devising new recipes. When she'd first agreed to judge amateur bakers, she'd imagined a tiny production watched only by serious foodies, and with a limited run. Had she known the show would become an international success, she never would have agreed to become so public a figure. Because Elspeth Peach had an important secret to keep. She was an excellent baker, but she was an even better witch.

Elspeth had made a foolish mistake. Baking made her happy, and she wanted to spread some of that joy to others. But she never envisaged how popular the series would become or how closely she'd be scrutinized by The British Witches Council, the governing body of witches in the UK. The council wielded great power, and any witch who didn't follow the rules was punished.

When she'd been unknown, she'd been able to fudge the borders of rule-following a bit. She always obeyed the main tenet of a white witch—do no harm. However, she wasn't so good at the dictates about not interfering with mortals without good reason. Now, she knew she was being watched very carefully, and she'd have to be vigilant. Still, as nervous as she was about her own position, she was more worried about her brand-new co-host.

Jonathon Pine was another famous British baker. His cookbooks rivaled hers in popularity and sales, so it shouldn't have been a surprise that he'd been chosen as her co-judge. Except that Jonathon was also a witch.

She'd argued passionately against the council's decision

to have him as her co-judge, but it was no good. She was stuck with him. And that put the only cloud in the blue sky of this lovely day.

To her surprise, she saw Jonathon approaching her. She'd imagined he'd be the type to turn up a minute before cameras began rolling. He was an attractive man of about fifty with sparkling blue eyes and thick, dark hair. However, at this moment he looked sheepish, more like a sulky boy than a baking celebrity. Her innate empathy led her to get right to the issue that was obviously bothering him, and since she was at least twenty years his senior, she said in a motherly tone, "Has somebody been a naughty witch?"

He met her gaze then. "You know I have. I'm sorry, Elspeth. The council says I have to do this show." He poked at a stone with the toe of his signature cowboy boot—one of his affectations, along with the blue shirts he always wore to bring out the color of his admittedly very pretty eyes.

"But how are you going to manage it?"

"I'm hoping you'll help me."

She shook her head at him. "Five best-selling books and a consultant to how many bakeries and restaurants? What were you thinking?"

He jutted out his bottom lip. "It started as a bit of a lark, but things got out of control. I became addicted to the fame."

"But you know we're not allowed to use our magic for personal gain."

He'd dug out the stone now with the toe of his boot, and his attention dropped to the divot he'd made in the lawn. "I know, I know. It all started innocently enough. This woman I met said no man can bake a proper scone. Well, I decided to show her that wasn't true by baking her the best scone she'd ever tasted. All right, I used a spell, since I couldn't bake a scone or anything else, for that matter. But it was a matter of principle. And then one thing led to another."

"Tell me the truth, Jonathon. Can you bake at all? Without using magic, I mean."

A worm crawled lazily across the exposed dirt, and he followed its path. She found herself watching the slow, curling brown body too, hoping. Finally, he admitted, "I can't boil water."

She could see that the council had come up with the perfect punishment for him by making the man who couldn't bake a celebrity judge. He was going to be publicly humiliated. But, unfortunately, so was she.

He groaned. "If only I'd said no to that first book deal. That's when the real trouble started."

Privately, she thought it was when he magicked a scone into being. It was too easy to become addicted to praise and far too easy to slip into inappropriate uses of magic. One bad move could snowball into catastrophe. And now look where they were.

When he raised his blue eyes to meet hers, he looked quite desperate. "The council told me I had to learn how to bake and come and do this show without using any magic at all." He sighed. "Or else."

"Or else?" Her eyes squinted as though the sun were blinding her, but really she dreaded the answer.

He lowered his voice. "Banishment."

She took a sharp breath. "As bad as that?"

He nodded. "And you're not entirely innocent either, you

know. They told me you've been handing out your magic like it's warm milk and cuddles. You've got to stop, Elspeth, or it's banishment for you, too."

She swallowed. Her heart pounded. She couldn't believe the council had sent her a message via Jonathon rather than calling her in themselves. She'd never used her magic for personal gain, as Jonathon had. She simply couldn't bear to see these poor, helpless amateur bakers blunder when she could help. They were so sweet and eager. She became attached to them all. So sometimes she turned on an oven if a baker forgot or saved the biscuits from burning, the custard from curdling. She'd thought no one had noticed.

However, she had steel in her as well as warm milk, and she spoke quite sternly to her new co-host. "Then we must make absolutely certain that nothing goes wrong this season. You will practice every recipe before the show. Learn what makes a good crumpet, loaf of bread and Victoria sponge. You will study harder than you ever have in your life, Jonathon. I will help you where I can, but I won't go down with you."

He leveled her with an equally steely gaze. "All right. And you won't interfere. If some show contestant forgets to turn their oven on, you don't make it happen by magic."

Oh dear. So they *did* know all about her little intervention in Season Two.

"And if somebody's caramelized sugar starts to burn, you do not save it."

Oh dear. And that.

"Fine. I will let them flail and fail, poor dears."

"And I'll learn enough to get by. We'll manage, Elspeth."

The word banishment floated in the air between them like the soft breeze.

"We'll have to."

～

Order your copy today! *The Great Witches Baking Show* is Book I in the series.

Vampire Knitting Club: Paranormal Cozy Mystery

Chapter and Curse - Book 2

A Spelling Mistake - Book 3

A Poisonous Review - Book 4

Toni Diamond Mysteries

Toni is a successful saleswoman for Lady Bianca Cosmetics in this series of humorous cozy mysteries.

Frosted Shadow - Book 1

Ultimate Concealer - Book 2

Midnight Shimmer - Book 3

A Diamond Choker For Christmas - A Holiday Whodunnit

Toni Diamond Mysteries Boxed Set: Books 1-4

The Almost Wives Club

An enchanted wedding dress is a matchmaker in this series of romantic comedies where five runaway brides find out who the best men really are!

The Almost Wives Club: Kate - Book 1

Secondhand Bride - Book 2

Bridesmaid for Hire - Book 3

The Wedding Flight - Book 4

If the Dress Fits - Book 5

The Almost Wives Club Boxed Set: Books 1-5

Take a Chance series

Meet the Chance family, a cobbled together family of eleven kids who are all grown up and finding their ways in life and love.

Chance Encounter - Prequel

Kiss a Girl in the Rain - Book 1

Iris in Bloom - Book 2

Blueprint for a Kiss - Book 3

Every Rose - Book 4

Love to Go - Book 5

The Sheriff's Sweet Surrender - Book 6

The Daisy Game - Book 7

Take a Chance Boxed Set: Prequel and Books 1-3

Abigail Dixon Mysteries: 1920s Cozy Historical Mystery

In 1920s Paris everything is très chic, except murder.

Death of a Flapper - Book 1

For a complete list of books, check out Nancy's website at
NancyWarrenAuthor.com

ABOUT THE AUTHOR

Nancy Warren is the USA Today Bestselling author of more than 100 novels. She's originally from Vancouver, Canada, though she tends to wander and has lived in England, Italy and California at various times. While living in Oxford she dreamed up The Vampire Knitting Club. Favorite moments include being the answer to a crossword puzzle clue in Canada's National Post newspaper, being featured on the front page of the New York Times when her book Speed Dating launched Harlequin's NASCAR series, and being nominated three times for Romance Writers of America's RITA award. She has an MA in Creative Writing from Bath Spa University. She's an avid hiker, loves chocolate and most of all, loves to hear from readers!

The best way to stay in touch is to sign up for Nancy's newsletter at NancyWarrenAuthor.com or www.facebook.com/groups/NancyWarrenKnitwits

To learn more about Nancy and her books
NancyWarrenAuthor.com

facebook.com/AuthorNancyWarren

twitter.com/nancywarren1

instagram.com/nancywarrenauthor

amazon.com/Nancy-Warren/e/B001H6NM5Q

goodreads.com/nancywarren

bookbub.com/authors/nancy-warren

Made in the USA
Coppell, TX
30 July 2022

80648833R00049